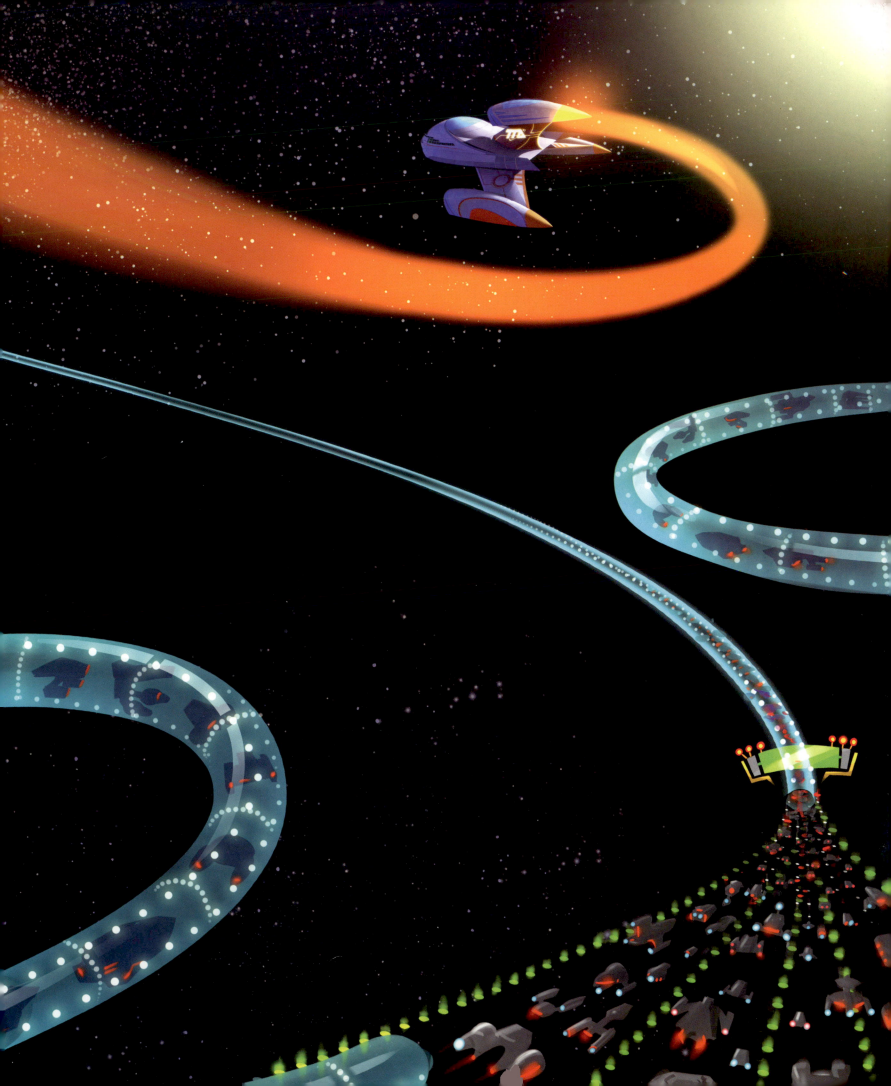

This edition published by Parragon Books Ltd in 2015

Parragon Books Ltd
Chartist House
15–17 Trim Street
Bath BA1 1HA, UK
www.parragon.com

ISBN 978-1-4748-3436-0

Printed in China

MIGHTY MERC!

Based on the episode written by Greg Johnson
Adapted by Sheila Sweeny Higginson

PaRragon

Bath • New York • Cologne • Melbourne • Delhi
Hong Kong • Shenzhen • Singapore • Amsterdam

It's not always easy living in the Stellosphere. A kid really needs a best friend when he's travelling around space with his family. That's why Miles is lucky to have Merc.

Merc may look like a strange, ostrich-shaped hunk of metal, but the Callisto family robot has feelings – real feelings.

Miles and Merc do everything together, from going on space missions to completing space chores. And when Merc sees something blastacular, like crystals floating past a star, there's only one person he wants to share it with!

Today Merc can't wait for the post to arrive. Miles knows Merc gets super-excited for Booster Bites!

Mr Xylon delivers a container of Booster Bites — and a special delivery package for Captain Callisto.

"What's in there?" Miles wonders, peeking inside.

Captain Callisto, otherwise known as Mum, places her hand on the scan screen.

The crate opens and reveals ... a robot replacement for Merc!

"Greetings, Callistos," it says. "I am Axel."

"This has to be a mistake," Miles says. "We already have the best robot in the universe!"

Mum checks in with Admirals Watson and Crick. It's no mistake. "Axel is the latest in Tomorrow Transit Authority technology," Watson tells her. "Your orders are to begin using him immediately. Just drop off Merc at the Tethoscape space station tomorrow."

Merc is heartbroken. He doesn't want to leave the Callistos!
But Miles has an idea. They have to prove to everyone that the
family robot is irreplaceable.

"Come on, Merc," Miles says. "I believe in you!"

Dad needs to load the heavy
weather station into the StarJetter.
That sounds like a job for Merc!

It turns out to be the perfect
job for Axel, though.

"I am programmed to assist
those less capable," Axel tells
them robotically.

Mum needs space barnacles scraped off the front windows.
Another perfect way for Merc to prove himself ... or maybe not.
When Merc accidentally bumps into the glass, Axel flies over.
He removes all the barnacles with a quick flash of his laser.

Later the Callistos all pile into the StarJetter.
They head to the planet Escalus for their next mission.

"Okay, Axel, let's see how fast you can set up the weather station," Dad says, challenging the new robot.

Axel whizzes into action and blows away Merc's record of seventeen minutes and nine seconds.

"We can't give up, Merc," Miles tells his robo-friend. "If you leave, who will I go on adventures with? Who will give me rides? Who will wake me up to show me rainbow rivers and stuff?"

Then Merc notices something odd. He chirps and shivers.

"You're right," Miles says. "It did just get colder."

Miles reports to his mum and dad, and Captain Callisto looks
at her screen to confirm the data.

"The nights get cold so fast here that everything freezes instantly,"
she explains to Miles.

Then she gasps. Loretta is out on the Terra-Skiff, exploring the cliffs!

Dad wants to rush out to save Loretta, but Axel blocks him. "Due to flash-freezing, rescue efforts would be too dangerous for the crew," the robot states.

Axel plugs into a terminal and the doors begin to close.
"My daughter is out there!" Captain Callisto cries. "I order you
to release control of this ship."

"Negative," Axel says robotically.

Merc can't believe his robot ears. Saving a member
of the Callisto family is worth any risk!

He lowers his metal head and slides through a hatch.
"Go, Merc!" Miles yells after him.

Merc races over the dark, freezing planet. He finds Loretta exploring the rocky ground and flings her onto his back.

Then he fires his boosters and weaves through the rocky landscape to get back to the StarJetter.

They are heading straight for the mini-spaceship, but the hatch is still closed!

Even though they are right outside, Axel will not open the hatch.

"Let them in, you hunk of junk!" Miles shouts.

"Negative," Axel replies. "That would endanger the rest of the crew."

Words won't stop Axel, but Captain Callisto knows about a switch on the control panel that will.

Once the robot is disabled, Miles throws his laserang at the hatch release button.

Merc and Loretta slide under the hatch, just in time!
Dad flies the StarJetter away as the planet freezes over. "I can't imagine the admirals will make us get rid of Merc now!" he says.

Back home on the Stellosphere, Mr Xylon comes to return Axel to Tomorrow. He also has another special delivery from Admirals Watson and Crick!

"It says, 'Nice job, Merc'," reads Mr Xylon as he holds out a tin of Booster Bites.

"You know how to protect this family, don't you, Merc?" Miles says.

"That's because he *is* family," Loretta agrees. "I wouldn't change a thing about our Merc."

And neither would Miles.

The End